This book is lovingly dedicated to our parents

Louise and Hugh Collett
and
Betty and Ken Hall

Thank you for introducing us to the magic of books
and to the beauty of nature.
We are forever grateful.

The photographs in the story were not staged or altered.

The exotic bird in the story, having escaped captivity, actually lived in the Cottonwoods
for several months. It then disappeared as suddenly as it had appeared.
We later learned that it was living happily with a nearby ranching family.

ISBN: 0-9722570-2-0
13-Digit: 978-0-9722570-2-2

Published by:

www.deertales.com

Book layout by Julie Melton, The Right Type Graphics (USA)

Printed in Hong Kong

2006

The Curious Adventure:

A Summer
Deer Tale

Karen Collett Wilson

By Karen Collett Wilson

Photography by Susan A. Zerga

2007

Susan Zerga

Did I ever tell you about the curious adventure that took place in our Cottonwoods not long ago? Gather near, and I'll tell you what happened.

It had been a long, hot summer. There had been day after day of brilliant Nevada-blue skies, with only the occasional cloud to block the searing sun.

Most of the deer in the Cottonwoods were spending the lazy days under the shady trees or by the banks of the snow-fed creek that skipped through the woods.

But one deer was tired of the endless heat and the tranquil beauty. He watched the leaves on the bushes and trees, hoping for a rustling movement that would signal a cooling breeze. He searched the skies for clouds that might mean that a noisy thunderstorm was on the way. He was restless and bored.

He was looking for adventure.

He asked the cat, who was sunning in the field, if he would like to go with him. But the cat was perfectly content and did not want to leave.

The nocturnal owl did not care a hoot about a daytime adventure.

The raccoon was waiting for the cool of evening before she prowled about.

The deer then asked the turkeys if they would go with him. They were excited about the idea for a moment but, soon became distracted, and forgot the question.

The beaver were too busy, even in the heat, building and repairing their dam, to bother with an adventure.

It was then that our restless friend saw another deer. This deer was not browsing under a shady bush. It did not appear to be sleepy or busy. It was simply standing in the woods, probably waiting for an adventure.

As he walked toward this deer, our friend began to have ideas about their upcoming adventure.

He imagined they would be led by a colorful bird, unlike any he had ever seen.

This exotic bird would take them to the nearby,
snow-capped mountains where the cool breezes blew.

Along the way, he imagined they would see new and unusual flowers…

...and new and unusual animals.

As he day-dreamed, our friend did not watch where he was going. He bumped right into the deer who was just standing in the woods. Curiously, that deer did not try to move out of the way. In fact, it did not act like an ordinary deer at all.

Hoping, at least, to get the strange deer to play,
our friend gave it a nudge…

…and then another. The unmoving deer was,
after all, not a real deer, and it could not run or play.
Instead, it just top-top-toppled over!

Startled by this surprising behavior, our friend ran as fast as he could to the safety of his deer family.

The once-restless deer was now hot and tired, and, after so much excitement, he decided he would wait for another day to go looking for an adventure.